PUFFIN

Cyril мc

Mary Hoffman was born in Eastleigh, Hants. She has been both a private tutor and a university lecturer for the Open University School of Education. She is now a freelance writer and educational consultant. Mary Hoffman is married and has three children.

For Howard Haigh

PUFFIN BOOKS

Published by the Penguin Group
Penguin Books Ltd, 27 Wrights Lane, London W8 5TZ, England
Penguin Books USA Inc., 375 Hudson Street, New York, New York 10014, USA
Penguin Books Australia Ltd, Ringwood, Victoria, Australia
Penguin Books Canada Ltd, 10 Alcorn Avenue, Toronto, Ontario, Canada M4V 3B2
Penguin Books (NZ) Ltd, 182–190 Wairau Road, Auckland 10, New Zealand

Penguin Books Ltd, Registered Offices: Harmondsworth, Middlesex, England

First published by Viking 1993
Published in Puffin Books 1994
1 3 5 7 9 10 8 6 4 2

Printed in England by Clays Ltd, St Ives plc

Cyril MC

BY

Mary
Hoffman

Illustrated by
Martin Chatterton

YO!

Here's the story of a *real cool dude*,
Who loved rhythm and music
the way you love food.

Cyril

was the name of this *unsung hero,*

The kind of name that made

him feel like a zero.

From the moment he was born,

he was BOPPING in his crib,

With a kicking beat,

that sounded street,

and rapping words ad lib.

And when he went to playgroup,
Cyril learned to

shake that floor.

He was moving
and a-**grooving**
like a Spanish matador.

He bopped,

hip-hopped,

he body-popped.

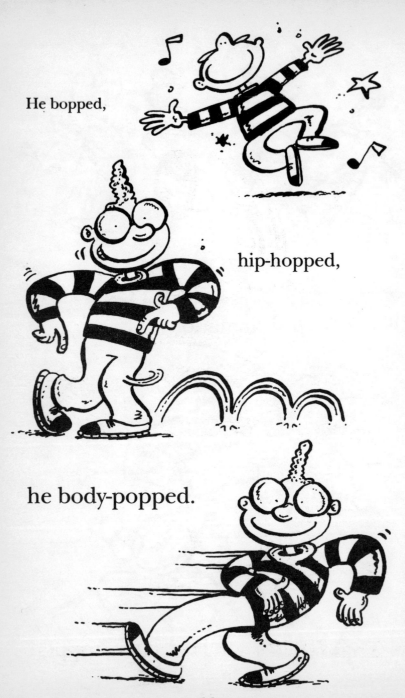

That **FUNKY** kid, he *never* stopped.

Cyril's *ragga rhythm*
drove his family quite

MAD.

Stop it!

cried his mother.

Quit! Enough!

yelled Dad.

He was Cyril, Cyril MC,
You've heard him on the
radio, seen him on TV.
Always on the move,
Always in the groove,
The kind of kid a parent
always wants to remove.

Cyril was a kid who
couldn't keep his body still,
Always *drumming* with his fingers
on the nearest window-sill.

At dinner time the food was always *jumping* on the table,

While Cyril's *rhythm solo* made the knives and forks unstable.

Wherever Cyril spent his time,
the joint was really *jumping*,
With his fingers *clicking*,
shoulders *shaking*,
little legs *a-pumping*.

The trouble really started

when young Cyril went to school.

His teachers all got *Hotter*

as the iceman got more

COOL.

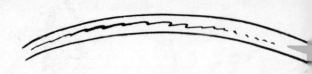

When Cyril slapped his thighs and
popped his cheeks in English class,
The teacher *threw* the book at him
and hit him on the...   ear.

He was Cyril, Cyril MC,
You've heard him on the
radio, seen him on TV.
Always on the move,
Always in the groove,
The kind of kid the teacher
always wants to reprove.

When he got to High School,
Cyril had a *real hard time*.
He could only learn a subject if
he put it into *rhyme*.

So History was a mystery
and Science a *closed book*.

If Cyril couldn't sing it,
it just didn't have that hook.

But there was just *one* subject where Cyril did the BEST.

In *every* music lesson,
he came TOP IN EVERY TEST.

His music teacher, **ARNOLD**,
was his number one fan,
And Cyril gave him five and said,
'Arnold, you're my man.'

He was Cyril, Cyril MC,
You've heard him on the
radio, seen him on TV.
Always on the move,
Always in the groove,
The kind of kid the teacher
always wants to remove.

Now Cyril has to choose

what to do for a career,

He turns down plumber,

 banker,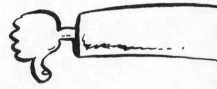

even civil engineer.

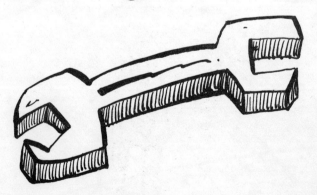

He shakes his head at everything
suggested by the master,
He clicks his fingers,
struts his stuff,
and starts to *talk much faster:*

'Sorry, mister, count me out,
I'll give those jobs a miss.
There's just one thing I gotta do,
and I don't mean no diss.'

I want to *rock*, I want to *roll*,
Need a job that's **full of soul**.

Have to *stomp*,
I have to *swagger*,
Need to *rap*,
hip-hop and *ragga*.

I must shake it, break it down,
Be the **hottest kid in town**.

That's right

says Cyril's teacher,

He could be a real main feature.
Don't put him in a bank,
Or stick him in a shop.
Don't make him drive a tank –
This kid was *born to bop*.

So Cyril and old Arnold

said goodbye to all at school.

They chose their mode,

they *hit the road*,

they walked out supercool.

Arnold found a studio that
made the proper sounds,
And Cyril made a record that
started earning pounds.

His head was full of lyrics,
his body full of song,
He couldn't wait to show them all
that they had got him wrong.

Now all the rest is history
and Cyril is a star,
Which only goes to show that
you should be *just what you are*.

Cyril is correct, Cyril has respect,
Cyril's up there – megabig –
what did you expect?

Now it's,

Cyril, sing
some more

Cyril, hit
the floor

Cyril, we all
love you

you're the
one that
we adore!

It's Cyril, Cyril MC,
You've heard him on the
radio, seen him on TV.
Always on the move,
Always in the groove,
The kind of man the deejays
say you've got to approve.